A Night at the Animal Shelter

MARK J. ASHER

A Night at the Animal Shelter

This is a work of fiction. Any references to real people, events, establishments, organizations, or locales are intended only to give the fiction a sense of reality and authenticity, and are used fictitiously. All other names, characters, and places, and all dialogue and incidents portrayed in this book are the product of the author's imagination.

ISBN-13: 978-1718959484
ISBN-10: 1718959486

Printed in the United States of America

Canine Characters

Maizie: Female Black Lab, 4 month old

Dutch: Male mixed breed, 11 year old

Raider: Male Pit Bull Terrier, 3 year old

Peg: Female Chihuahua, 6 year old

Georgie: Female Golden Retriever, 7 year old

The old dog sat with his nose pressed against the cold steel cage, staring out at the hillside across the way. As the final flickers of sunlight began to fade, he watched a blonde-haired woman jogging along one of the trails with her yellow Lab.

To a person the hillside wouldn't merit much thought—it was one in a valley filled with many. But to a dog confined in a small sliver of space, it had everything to long for: a human companion to be with, paths to explore, an open field to run through, earthly delights to smell, and squirrels and birds to chase.

Although only one side of the Blithedale Animal Shelter faced the incline, all of the dogs—either while taking a walk around the rectangular building or playing in one of the outdoor pens—couldn't help but notice the activity on it.

The old dog continued gazing out, following a hawk as it soared through the steely blue sky, until he heard the sound of his cage door opening. As quickly as his tender joints would move him, Dutch walked the short length of the enclosure to greet Ginny Collins, a middle-aged employee with a worn but warm disposition.

"Dinnertime sweet boy," she said, putting down a bowl of kibble and replenishing his water.

Dutch picked out a few pieces of food and spit them onto the cement ground before beginning to dig in.

"I brought you an extra blanket," Ginny told the dog while she tidied up his sparse surroundings. "It's going to be one cold Christmas Eve."

When Dutch finished eating, he sauntered up beside Ginny. She stroked his brown, thick coat several times and then wrapped her arms around his body and squeezed him tight.

"I promised I'd get you out of here by the holidays," Ginny whispered in his ear. "I'm sorry."

When she released the old dog, tears were streaming down her face. Dutch stared at her earnestly for a moment and then leaned over and reached for her glasses, where there was a speck of wet dog food on a piece of tape that connected the arm of her glasses to the frame.

"Whatcha doing silly dog?" she asked him, wiping her tears away and laughing. "You may be old, but I don't think you'd have any use for these."

With her knees on the ground and her legs behind her, Ginny cradled the dog's head in her hands. "I wonder what breed of dog you are," she pondered aloud. "A friend of mine would probably call you a BHD for Big Hairy Dog. Whatever you are, you got a bad break Dutch. Life isn't fair sometimes, is it big guy?"

Tired of standing, Dutch retreated to his bed, lay down on his side, and lifted his hind leg up slightly.

"Nothing that a belly rub can't help huh?" Ginny asked, smiling down on him.

While Ginny rubbed and gently rocked Dutch's body back and forth, the old dog let out grunts of approval. Unbeknownst to either of them, a tall male shelter employee was looking on from outside of the cage.

"You're so sweet with these dogs," Tom finally said. "They love you Ginny."

"Oh, I didn't see you," Ginny replied, turning around and looking up. "Well, they deserve it. Besides, tomorrow is a hard day for them."

"You think they know it's Christmas?" Tom asked incredulously.

"Maybe," Ginny answered with a laugh. "Even if they don't, there won't be any visitors or volunteers here tomorrow—just some of the staff—and they'll be lonely."

"I can't believe the rush we had on dogs for that

promotion," Tom replied. "About two-thirds are gone…a few others went home with volunteers for the holiday. I moved the remaining ones to this side so everyone is together."

"People shouldn't need a sale," Ginny responded. "These beautiful creatures offer love for freedom Tom. Even Walmart can't beat that deal."

"I agree," Tom replied. "Okay, well it looks like I'm out of here. You have yourself a nice Christmas Ginny."

"I will Tom. Have a good night," Ginny said, standing up.

"Everyone is rushing to leave, so you may be the last one left."

"No problem, I'll lock up."

After Tom waved and walked off, Ginny turned back to Dutch. "I'm going to check on some of your friends," she said, patting the dog's head. "But first, I'm going to turn off this music.

If I hear *Silent Night* one more time, I'm going to go insane."

Once she silenced the small boom box by the entrance to the building, Ginny walked back and entered the cage next to Dutch's. She was immediately ambushed by a rambunctious female black Lab. The puppy's overzealous greeting didn't faze Ginny.

"Crazy Maizie, that's what we'll call you," she said. "Yes, I'm going to give you some food sweet girl, but you gotta stop jumping up on people like that. The woman who turned you in said you weren't the dog she hoped for after sending you to the most expensive dog academy in the Valley. But then again, she also said you smelled. Maybe like a dog? People…"

After Maizie scarfed down her dinner, Ginny stroked the puppy's ears and talked to her.

"I know it's hard to be locked up when you

have all that energy," she said. "But you'll be free soon. We just need to find you the right owner and you'll be just fine."

After visiting for a few more minutes, Ginny gave Maizie a stuffed toy, kissed her on top of the head and left the cage. When the dog heard the door shut, she looked up at Ginny as if she were being unexpectedly abandoned after a long love affair.

"Oh come on now," Ginny said, smiling at her. "It's not *that* bad—you're okay Maizie."

The next dog on Ginny's rounds was a shorthaired, tan Chihuahua with three legs and a missing eye. The dog stood on her bed slightly trembling, as she watched Ginny step inside of her cage.

"Hello Peg," Ginny said, sitting down on the ground cross-legged. "You seem like you're doing a little better today. There's just a few of you here tonight, so it shouldn't be as crazy."

Feeling safe with Ginny, Peg walked over and crawled onto her lap. Ginny cradled the dog and slowly stroked her coat from head to tail, over and over again.

"I bet you'd like this royal treatment all night long, wouldn't you Peg?" she asked, as the dog squinted with pleasure. "Unfortunately, I have to get going…so you eat your dinner and have a good night. Okay Sweetie?"

After Ginny re-adjusted Peg's fleece coat, she got up and walked to the next space over. There was a regal Golden Retriever patiently sitting in the front of the cage, awaiting her arrival.

"There's our Golden Girl," Ginny said, as she turned the door latch. "It's time for some good stuff Georgie." The dog swooshed her tail back and forth and rubbed up alongside Ginny's leg.

"I'm not worried about you," Ginny told

Georgie, reaching over to rub her head and put down her food. "If that couple hadn't put a hold on you and then changed their mind, you'd be gone by now. So we'll just keep your spirits up, until someone else comes along."

After Ginny left Georgie's cage, she walked into the storage room at the end of the building, opposite the entrance, and made a few notations on a whiteboard. Then she grabbed her jacket and purse and walked down the row of cages to leave. As she passed by each dog, she waved and spoke to them. When she got to the last one—a black Pit Bull Terrier with patches of white and a forlorn expression—she stopped.

"Look at those Scooby Doo ears," Ginny said, smiling and putting down her purse. "You got lots of food and love already Raider, but I can't leave without saying goodbye."

The dog waited anxiously by his cage door for

Ginny to enter. Once she walked inside and knelt down, he slurped her face repeatedly.

"Sweet kisses, I love those sweet kisses," she told him. "It's hard to believe that some people walk by your cage and see a big bad Pit Bull, instead of a fur baby with a heart of gold. Huh Raider? Everyone thinks tiny dogs are cute and sweet as pie, but some can be real bitches. And a breed that's been stereotyped to be as mean as the devil can have some of the nicest dogs."

Ginny visited with Raider until his tail was wagging again, and then she finally left the building and walked out into the brisk nighttime air.

After taking a few steps she stopped, grabbed the gloves from her coat pocket and put them on. Once she got past the chain link fence that enclosed the shelter building and the exercise pens, Ginny closed the gate behind her and fastened the padlock.

By this time Dutch was standing in the outdoor portion of his cage, watching the headlights from Ginny's car come on and slowly pull away. Once she was out of sight, the old dog turned and stared at the hillside for a few moments before retreating to his bed.

Inside the shelter the other dogs continued to stir in their cages, looking toward the entrance, hoping for more human interaction. Once they realized their wait was in vain, they joined Dutch in settling in for another night.

All except for one.

"Who's going stir crazy over there?" Dutch asked, lying on his side.

"I–I can't stand being coo–cooped up like this," Maizie replied, anxiously pacing back and forth.

"Are you the black Lab puppy who came in this morning?" Dutch asked.

"Yes..." Maizie answered while darting from the inside to the outside of her cage through a small opening in the dividing wall.

"You'll settle down," the old dog reassured her. "It takes a while."

"How did you end up here?" Peg, the Chihuahua, asked the puppy in a high-pitched voice.

"I don't know..." Maizie answered, now standing in the front of her cage. "My owner told me I was a bad dog. Then she put me in the car and brought me here."

"I'm here for no fault of my own," Georgie, the Golden Retriever said with a hint of arrogance. "But I heard Ginny talking to you and it sounded like you have some issues."

"Did your owner smack you?" Raider, the Pit Bull Terrier asked before Maizie could respond.

"One time," Maizie replied, panting.

"Do you remember what you were doing right before she hit you?" Raider asked.

"She's just a puppy," Dutch interjected. "How's she supposed to remember?"

"I wish I was young again," Georgie said. "I miss all that attention. People still tell me I'm a beautiful dog, but nothing gets a human more excited than a cute puppy."

"You have nothing to complain about," Raider responded. "You heard what Ginny said—a Golden Retriever like you will be out of here before any of us. A Pit Bull like me has to worry every day about being taken out back to the Doom Room if someone doesn't come for me quick."

"I hope you're right Raider…about me anyway," Georgie replied. "But I'm almost eight years old and no matter what breed you are, gray is a human's least favorite color when it comes to adopting a dog."

"I'm not getting older—I'm OLD," Dutch said. "But let's not depress ourselves. I want to hear what happened to the young pup."

Maizie stopped her incessant motion for a second and asked, "What does 'That's it' mean?"

"It could mean a lot of things," Dutch answered. "It depends on what you were doing when your owner said it."

"I was playing with my rope toy and decided to put it on her lap so I could be close to her while I chewed it," the puppy replied.

"Don't feel bad about that, nobody likes to play alone," Raider responded. "Did she say anything else to you?"

"Before that she said, 'Get that disgusting, soggy thing off of me,'" the puppy replied innocently.

"So what did you do?" Dutch asked.

"I took the rope toy and jumped on the couch and buried it beneath the pillows."

"Well, *that* was probably *it*," Dutch responded.

"You just need some training," Peg told Maizie. "After my first real owners took me to doggie school, I calmed down a lot and learned how to behave."

"Don't fill the young pup's head with rubbish," Dutch said. "Every smart dog knows the idea is to train your owner *before* they train you."

"How do you do that?" the puppy asked the old dog.

"Once you get them in the habit of doing what you want them to do, when they don't comply you give them an incredulous look. Humans respond to guilt. It's worked like a charm for every owner I've had."

Dutch stood up to reposition himself on his bed before continuing. "Training a human is easy—understanding them is the hard part. I mean who collects their best smelling stuff all week long in a can in the kitchen and then puts it outside to be taken away? Then, to top it off, they have the nerve to get mad at you for helping yourself to something they don't even want."

"Humans are tricky Maizie, you have to be careful," Raider offered the puppy. "They'll make dog training seem like fun, but it's a ruse. You start out with lots of treats and you end up with lots of commands."

"And one more thing," Dutch added. "Never go potty until you're ready to turn around and go home, because some humans like to make that the end of your walk."

"Dutch, if you're such a smart dog, then how did you end up here?" Georgie asked sharply.

"My owner died," the old dog said sadly. "We were taking our regular midday walk around the block...he pulled me over to the curb, grabbed his chest and stopped breathing."

"Oh no!" Georgie replied. "That's so horrible."

"Joe was my third owner and he was a dog's dream," Dutch said. "I wish I could have lived out my life with him. Old as I am now, I might not make it out of here."

"Someone will give you a home," Peg said positively. "When I used to be across from you, before they moved us, I always saw people stop by your cage."

"Maybe so, but all I know is since I've been here I've only had one real chance to be adopted," Dutch replied. "It was this sweet, older lady. She sat on the ground and petted me for a really long time. I thought for sure, *this is the one.* Then a few minutes later, she called over one of the volunteers, handed her my leash, and said, "I'm sorry, I just can't do it."

"I *did* have a good home," Raider, the Pit Bull Terrier said regretfully. "I lived with a college student named Mattie. We shared an apartment by the University with two other girls. Mattie loved me more than anything, but when her parents found out about me they said she couldn't have a Pit Bull. That I was dangerous and I could turn on her at any second."

"I'm sorry Raider," Peg said sympathetically. "If it makes you feel any better, I spent the first two years of my life in a dirty, rusty cage much smaller than this one, with three other dogs. The people who ran the place gave us no walks, no treats, and no love. All they wanted us for was to make puppies."

"That's so sad," Georgie replied. "How did you ever get out of there?"

"A rescue group discovered that the people were running a puppy mill and closed it down. They're the ones who found me my first real home," Peg answered. "I was a happy dog, living with my family, until one day someone left the front door open and I ran out into the street and got hit by a truck."

"No!" Georgie cried.

"That's how I lost most of my back right leg," Peg continued. "I'm lucky I didn't lose my life."

"How did a little dog like you survive something like that?" Raider asked.

"The guy who hit me rushed me to an emergency Vet. The doctors there were so nice… they saved me," Peg replied. "But when I was ready to go home, no one from my family came to pick me up."

"My old owner, Joe, used to say *some humans just aren't that human*," Dutch responded. "Sad, but true."

"Well, my story is upsetting too, but I didn't do anything wrong," Georgie said defensively.

"Just tell us and we'll be the judge of that," Raider replied, matter-of-factly.

"I was born in a litter of seven puppies at one of the most prestigious Golden Retriever breeders in the country. They called us *The Spectacular Seven*," Georgie explained. "I was the first one to be adopted by a wonderful family with two kids and a big backyard."

"Sounds like a dream so far," Raider remarked.

"It was for seven years," Georgie replied. "But once the kids left for college the parents, Rob and Danielle, began to fight all the time. Then one day, out of the blue, they started packing up everything in the house. Next thing I knew they were both hugging me and crying and saying goodbye."

"Well, what happened?" Dutch asked. "Why didn't one of them keep you?"

"I don't know," Georgie said sadly. "I just know that I didn't do anything wrong. I'm a perfectly trained dog. I don't beg, I know more than ten commands, and I can do lots of tricks."

"Well, I guess none of them includes making your owners keep you," Raider said harshly.

"That's mean," Peg replied, coming to the Golden Retriever's defense.

"Don't feel bad Georgie, most times dogs are the last to know and the first to go," Dutch said. "I bet you didn't do anything wrong."

"Thank you Dutch," Georgie replied.

"Someone let me out of here," Maizie interjected, still worked up. "A dog shouldn't be left in a small cage for so long."

"That's for sure," Raider replied.

"You'll be alright," Peg offered. "If a nervous wreck like me can adjust, any dog can."

"Tomorrow–tomorrow someone will come and take me out of here," Maizie said, standing still for a second and staring blankly at her cage door.

"It's not going to happen—tomorrow is

Christmas," Raider replied. "That means the shelter is closed."

"Gosh, this sure is a long way from being home for the holidays," Georgie said.

"More like hell for the holidays," Raider responded.

"Last Christmas my family got me a brand new cushy bed and a big basket filled with treats," Georgie told the group.

"My family never got me a gift for Christmas," Peg replied. "But at least I had a home and that's the best gift any dog can have."

"I love the smells of Christmas," Georgie said. "The tree, the presents, the guests, the ham, the turkey, the Apple pie."

"I like falling asleep in front of a crackling fire," the old dog replied.

"Have any of you ever wished you were human?" Raider asked the other dogs.

"Not me," Dutch replied. "From what I've seen it's mostly work and worry with occasional moments of joy. I'd rather be happy as a dog any day."

"I love being a dog, but I hate being here and waiting to see who my next owner will be," Peg said.

"Just imagine, if you were a human you could pick any dog you wanted," Raider responded.

"That's true," Peg replied. "We're the only family member a human gets to choose."

"And most times we're the only ones they don't fight with," Raider responded.

"I just want to be free again," Maizie chimed in, trying to get comfortable on her bed.

"We all do young pup," Dutch replied. "Even when your bones are brittle and your muzzle is gray like mine, you still have the spirit of a puppy."

"I miss sticking my head out of the car window

on the ride to the dog park," Georgie said. "I love all the smells from the farms along the way."

"I need to run and play and dig and chew," Maizie said.

"Dutch, what do you miss most about not having a home?" Raider asked.

"Sunspots and soft beds" the old dog replied. "The sun shines on that hillside all day long, but it goes down right before it reaches our cages. And the staff seems to like these beds because they're easy to clean, but they're like sleeping on lawn furniture."

"Nothing compares to your owner's bed…I used to love Mattie's," Raider replied. "Dog beds are comfy, but they don't have the scent of the person you love."

"I wish Ginny or one of the volunteers would take us to that hillside," Georgie said. "I stare at it every day, wishing I was over there running around, chasing squirrels."

"My owner took me for a walk on *that* hillside the first day she got me," Maizie said.

"Being locked in a cage makes you wonder where the saying *lucky dog* comes from," Raider said, feeling defeated.

"I guess it's because we get to sleep and play all day," Peg answered.

"Yeah well, I don't think any of us feels real lucky right now," Raider responded.

In an instant the conversation ceased and every one of the dogs, except for Dutch, rushed to the front of their cages.

"What was *that*?" Georgie asked, letting out a round of barks.

"I heard something," Peg replied, after yapping uncontrollably.

"Peg, you'd bark if a feather fell," Dutch said from his bed. "It's probably nothing."

"Somebody's here to let us out!" the puppy

cried, spinning around in circles of joy.

"I think it was just a gust of wind," Raider replied, calming down.

For a while longer the dogs continued to stare toward the entrance, wagging their tails and intermittently barking, clinging to the hope that someone might appear. When it didn't happen, Georgie, Peg, and Raider went back to their beds and soon drifted off to sleep.

The shelter was in darkness now with the only light coming from the moon. Other than an occasional gust of wind or the sounds of the old building adjusting to the dropping temperature, the night was quiet.

While the others rested, Maizie sat at the rear of her cage and stared at the hillside. She pictured herself being chased by a pack of dogs through the tall brush, her heart racing and wind rushing through her fur. The puppy was still confused by the concept of being free one moment and caged the next.

Just as she was about to walk back inside, Maizie detected a dart of motion out of the corner of her eye. Turning her head quickly, at first she didn't see anything. But a second later she discovered what it was. A white cat was taking an evening stroll behind one of the outdoor pens. Maizie began whimpering like mad before jumping up and digging her claws into the metal grill of her cage.

"What?" Raider cried, immediately springing from his bed and quickly seeing Maizie's view.

Within seconds, Georgie and Peg were also standing at the rear of their cages, looking to see what was going on. Once they realized it was a cat, neither of them reacted the way Maizie had.

"She's cute," Georgie said, slowly walking her front paws forward, until she was lying down.

"I like cats," Peg said while Maizie and Raider continued to stare down the feline. "I used to live with a beautiful one named Nikita. Unfortunately she got eaten by coyotes."

Hearing all of the commotion, Dutch finally got up from his bed to see what the fuss was about.

"Well, lookie, lookie," the old dog said, recognizing the source of the excitement. "We have a visitor."

"Call it what it is—dessert," Raider responded.

"You're not kidding," Dutch replied.

"I don't know how many lives that cat has left, but I'd sure like to take one of them," Raider said.

The cat slowly sauntered over toward the row of dog cages like a confident burlesque dancer. Maizie, Raider, and Dutch became more agitated—jumping and whimpering—with every step she took. The cat remained unfazed, stopping occasionally and glancing over at the boisterous dogs as if to say, *Oh you silly dogs.*

"It's nothing to go on like that about," Georgie declared, standing up.

"I wish she could come and spend the night with me," Peg said. "I miss having someone in here to cuddle with since Bennie got adopted."

"I hate to say this," Dutch replied, turning away from the cat who was now past the row of cages and out of view. "But I think that dog might come back."

"How can you say that?" Peg asked. "Everyone was so crazy for that cute Chihuahua."

"Well, did you see who adopted him? A young couple expecting a baby," Dutch said, answering his own question. "That cute little dog will be their pride and joy, until their *real* pride and joy comes along. Then it'll become nothing more than a neglected nuisance. Trust me...it happened to me when I was just a puppy. I was in heaven until that ugly toddler replaced me. From the second that baby could coo my owners treated me as if I were a cat! The only good thing about that drooling mess was I liked cleaning up after him."

"That's not always the case," Georgie replied. "The couple that adopted me had two young kids and I *was* part of the family. I had a bed in every room and a special spot on the couch. I even had my own popcorn bowl with *my* name on it for movie nights."

"But the kids were already there when you were adopted. That's different," Dutch replied.

"I just wish they never left for college," Georgie responded. "Then maybe I'd still have a home."

"I think for my next owner I want a single female who works from home," Peg said. "Someone who just got out of a long relationship and is tired of men. That way she can give all of her time and love to ME."

"I don't know about that," Raider replied. "The owner I had before Mattie, Warren, worked from home and it was nothing but a tease. I thought for sure I'd get lots of long walks and plenty of playtime, but all he did, day and night, was work. I'd get so bored lying around, waiting for him to stop, that sooner or later I'd go stand right next to his desk and intensely stare at him. He wouldn't even realize I was there. Then I'd start whimpering. When that didn't work, I'd paw at his arm. Finally, he'd turn to me annoyed and anxiously say, 'What? What do you want? A treat? More water? What?' Reluctantly, he'd push away from his desk, take me out for a walk, and then we'd play our favorite game."

"Boy, I hope it was worth it after all of that," Dutch interjected.

"It was!" Raider excitedly replied. "He'd put a big piece of foam on the floor and throw a tennis ball against it. The game was for me to try to intercept it with my paws before it flew up in the air. Whenever I blocked the ball, I'd strut around with it in my mouth, until Warren chased me through the house. He'd be so happy, acting like an oversized kid. But then he'd think of something, go back to his desk and start working again."

"It's torture when you know they can be doing better things with their time and they choose to work instead," Dutch offered. "Sometimes I think humans aren't fully developed. Because if they were they'd know there's only three things worth doing in life: playing, eating, and sleeping."

Raider gave himself a good shake, and then announced, "So for my next owner I wouldn't mind a master chef who cooks all day long and makes me their official taste tester."

"I just want the family I had back," Georgie said mournfully.

"I don't care who adopts me—anybody with a leash and some food is fine," Maizie said.

"The puppy has the right attitude," Dutch replied. "Whoever adopts any of us, we'll adjust. After all, nobody adapts to humans, with all of their foibles, like a dog does."

"I wonder if that's the reason they love us so much?" Peg asked.

"I don't know," Raider replied. "But as long as there's places like this still around, I'd say it's not enough love."

"When I lived with my family, I remember watching this program on TV about jails," Georgie told the group. "They're just like shelters, but for humans who do really bad things."

"To end up here all you need is an uncaring family," Peg said.

"Or be the wrong breed," Raider added.

"Or be too playful," Maizie said.

"What they need is a special jail for people who mistreat their dogs," Raider suggested.

"That's a good idea," Dutch replied. "They can use the cages we're in."

Soon the conversation died down and before long all of the dogs were sound asleep. Maizie's head dangled uncomfortably off of her bed and her body was contorted in an ungainly position. With the puppy finally resigned to rest, it seemed as if all would be quiet until the morning came.

But a few hours later, the dogs heard a loud thud. They sprang from their beds startled and rushed to the front of their cages again.

This time it wasn't the wind—it was Ginny. She had come through the entrance and fallen down.

The sight of her set the dogs off on a barking blitzkrieg that reverberated loudly throughout the building.

"First my car dies on me, now I can't walk right," Ginny said to herself, standing up. The dogs watched her intently, excitedly wagging their tails as she made her way towards them.

"Yeah, I'm back Raider…Georgie…Peg… Maizie…Dutch," she said as she opened their cage doors, setting the dogs free.

The dogs joyfully danced around Ginny and exchanged whiffs and wags with one another. While Peg clamored for Ginny to pick her up, Georgie and Dutch playfully argued over the rights to a nearby Kong toy. Maizie and Raider romped along the cement walkway between the two rows of cages.

"I couldn't sleep," Ginny told the Chihuahua, nuzzling the dog to her face. "So I thought I'd come be with you guys. Is that okay sweet pea?"

It didn't take long for the freed dogs to gravitate toward the rear of the building and begin milling around in the storage room. Looking up and spotting them, Ginny called the group back over to where she and Peg were standing.

"C'mon guys…over here," she said, signaling with a tilt of her head. "I'll get some treats for everybody in just a minute. We also need some blankets. You guys have fur coats on, but I'm cold. And so is precious Peg."

The dogs slowly made their way back to Ginny. Once everyone was congregated together, she told them to stay while she and Peg went to gather what they needed.

Once they returned, Ginny spread several blankets down on the ground and lured each of the dogs onto one of them with a treat. "I bet you guys are surprised to see me in the middle of the night," she said to the dogs gathered around her in a semi-circle, with the exception of Peg, who was bundled in a blanket on her lap.

For a half hour or so, Ginny told stories to the dogs, including how she came to volunteer at the shelter after her husband had died.

"This is David," she said, pulling a photograph from her bag. "We were married for 22 years and had two beautiful girls together. They're grown now, living across the country with families of their own. David's been gone for 10 years now, but I think about him every day. Especially on this one."

Ginny silently stared at the photograph, while she slowly stroked Peg's coat.

"It was on a Christmas Eve that he died suddenly from a heart attack," she continued, as tears welled up in her eyes. "I didn't think I could exist without him. My kids and I gave one another strength and comfort, but eventually they had to go back to school and get on with their lives. My friends were angels, never leaving my side, helping me get from one day to the next. But time moves on, and you're supposed to move with it. I tried, but I just couldn't. Soon my friends started saying things like, 'David is gone, it's time to start living again; holding on to the past is killing you.' But the past is the only place I felt safe. I didn't want to let go of it.

"Anyway, one day on a whim I came here to see about adopting a dog. You were all like me, abandoned and wounded, but you showered me with love and began to slowly fill the empty hole in my heart. Instead of just taking one dog home, I ended up committing my life to saving as many of you as I could. I'll forever be grateful to dogs for giving me a place to put my pain and a purpose for living again."

Ginny cuddled Peg to her face, and tears rolled onto the dog's fur. Maizie sprang up and came over to give Ginny more than a few licks on her nose. As she pulled away from the excitable puppy, a smile formed on Ginny's lips and her mood instantly changed. "Okay everyone," she announced enthusiastically, lifting up her head. "Now that I've bored you with my stories, let's go outside and play!"

Once they exited the building, the dogs pranced around with one another and roamed in and out of the pens, while Ginny sat and stared at the moon. Soon she got up and interacted with the dogs, tossing them tennis balls and jostling with them for toys. When the dogs had had their fill of playing, and Ginny was getting cold and tired, she called the group to follow her back inside.

Once Ginny put away the blankets, she gave each of the dogs a treat and put them back into their cages. Maizie refused at first, eluding Ginny a couple of times, but the puppy eventually relented.

"Okay guys," Ginny called out to the group, picking up her bag off of the ground. "Be good for Tom tomorrow. Merry Christmas!"

After she padlocked the gate, Ginny walked through the parking lot and opened the front door to the administration building. She put her bag on a desk behind the counter and pulled out her cell phone to call a cab. Before someone on the other end could pick up, she ended the call, put her phone away, and went to lie down on a cot in a room at the end of the hallway.

Inside the shelter, the dogs were still standing in front of their cages, glancing toward the entrance. Like always, they longed for more attention but they were less agitated as a result of their unexpected visitor.

"I guess she's not coming back," Peg finally said in a sorrowful voice.

"I wish she would have taken me with her," Maizie replied.

"If every human had a heart like Ginny's none of us would be here," Dutch told the group.

"I love surprises," Georgie said. "That was fun!"

"I'm happy she came to see us, but I hate when she calls me *Raider*," the Pit Bull Terrier shared.

"What else would she call you?" Dutch asked.

"Sal...that's what Mattie called me before someone here decided to change my name," Raider replied. "It's challenging enough getting adopted as a large, black Pit Bull without a name like *Raider*."

"Well, you could be a three-legged dog named *Peg*," the Chihuahua responded.

"But you're small and cute," Raider replied.

"I love my name," Georgie interjected. "My family used to call me *Georgie Girl* or *Gorgeous Georgie*."

"You're a pure breed Golden Retriever," Dutch responded. "If your name was *Killer* or *Piddle Poo* you'd still get adopted."

Eventually all of the dogs, except for Maizie, retreated to their beds and fell asleep. Still restless, the black Lab puppy paced back and forth between the indoor and outdoor sections of her cage. She would stand and gaze out into the night for a few moments, and then walk back inside and stare at the empty cage across the way. On one of her rounds something unusual caught her eye.

"Look!" she cried out. "My cage door…it's not closed all the way!"

"Really?" Raider asked surprised, opening his eyes. "Are you sure?"

"Poor puppy," Dutch lamented. "She's so stressed out that she's starting to see things."

In an instant Dutch saw a flash of black fur dash past his cage door, heading in the direction of the storage room. Seconds later he heard Maizie rummaging around, followed by the sound of a box of treats spilling to the ground. All of the dogs began to bark and whimper.

"Hey young pup!" Dutch called out. "Don't forget about your friends."

But Maizie couldn't be bothered—she was too busy gobbling up one treat after another, as if she were playing an edible game of Pac-Man.

Once she finished off the remaining treats, the puppy sniffed around the room in search of more food. Not finding anything else, she ran past the other dogs on her way to the entrance of the building.

"You little runt," Raider yelled as she zipped by his cage. "Let us out too."

Maizie sniffed the air coming from the crack beneath the door, and then jumped up and pawed at the knob. After several unsuccessful tries at prying the door open, she went back over to the dogs, who were still worked up and making noise.

Arriving in front of Dutch's cage, Maizie stood on her hind legs and swatted the horizontal door latch with her front paws. The old dog looked on like an excited puppy, eagerly anticipating being freed. On Maizie's second try, Dutch's cage door popped opened and moved forward.

"You did it!" he cried, stepping over the metal cross bar and greeting Maizie.

The next closest cage was Peg's, and seeing the two dogs celebrating on the walkway sent her into a barking frenzy.

"She's not going to stop that yapping until you let her out," Dutch said to the puppy.

Maizie walked a few feet over, leaped up and pawed at Peg's cage, until it opened. The Chihuahua quickly scampered out and jumped up to give Dutch and Maizie kisses.

"Don't tell me the Pit Bull is last again," Raider said, anxiously pacing in front of his cage door.

"Stop complaining," Dutch said as Maizie went over and worked her magic again.

Once Raider was free, he immediately made a bee-line for the entrance. Like Maizie, he sniffed below the door before jumping up and seeing if there was a way to get out. No matter how many times he tried, he didn't have any luck.

Georgie was the last dog left in her cage, but after Maizie opened her door the Golden Retriever didn't budge. She just lay quietly on her bed.

Maizie stood for a second waiting for Georgie to get up, and then quickly ran off to join Dutch, Raider, and Peg, who were in the storage room busy sniffing around. Once they realized the puppy had done a thorough job of cleaning up the spilt treats, the dogs wandered in and out of several of the empty cages, drinking from water bowls and searching for any morsels of food they could find.

After exploring for a little while, Peg returned to the area where the dogs had been locked up and saw Georgie still lying on her side, uninterested in leaving her cage.

"What's wrong?" she asked her. "Don't you want to come out?"

"I'm trained to follow the lead of my owners or whoever is taking care of me," Georgie replied. "I don't want to misbehave."

"Misbehave?" Raider repeated, bounding up beside Peg. "That's what your owners did by packing up and leaving *you* behind."

"I still love my family," Georgie replied softly.

"You're a beautiful dog," Peg told the Golden Retriever. "Another family will adopt you soon and give you a new home. I just know it."

Georgie didn't respond, she just stared straight ahead.

It didn't take long for the dogs to acclimate to their new arrangement. Raider and Dutch found suitable spots in the storage room in which to lie down. Peg climbed onto Georgie's bed and snuggled close to the Golden Retriever. Maizie continued to roam around the building, putting her nose into every nook and cranny she could reach. Once she exhausted every possibility, the puppy decided to curl up on the cement floor in front of Georgie's open cage.

With everyone settled the building fell silent, and in a short time all of the dogs were asleep again.

The tranquility lasted for almost an hour. That's when Maizie decided to get up and walk into the storage room. With nothing new to discover on the ground, she hopped onto a large storage box.

From there she leap-frogged on to a desk that blocked the rear exit of the building. After sniffing some papers and licking a small spot of spilt coffee, Maizie jumped back to the ground where she found a smidgen of a treat. While she sniffed around for more beneath the desk, she smelled a sliver of air coming from the outside.

The puppy wandered over and pressed her nose against the tight seam of the door. Intrigued, she stuck her snout up against it another time and then scratched at it with her right paw. The door let out a tiny squeak.

By now Raider was on his way toward Maizie, and Dutch was standing on his bed, cocking his head at the sound the door had made. Once Raider reached the puppy he nuzzled himself between her and the door, and the door opened a crack. After another thrust forward by the dogs, they were outside of the building.

Dutch let out a bark and wagged his tail before heading as quickly as he could to join them. When the old dog got outside, Maizie and Raider were already running wild in the nighttime air.

The pen gates were open from earlier and Maizie rushed inside one of them and grabbed an oversized tennis ball. Dutch went into the next one over and relieved himself. Then he walked along the concrete pathway, until he met up with Raider at the padlocked gate, which led to the parking lot. Looking up, the dogs realized they wouldn't be able to go any further.

Raider and Dutch turned away and scrounged around for a while longer, investigating an area behind one of the pens, which had a small shed, and sniffing the trash cans on the grounds. Eventually both dogs went back inside the shelter. Maize stayed outside continuing to explore.

When Raider and Dutch made it back to

Georgie's cage, the Golden Retriever and the Chihuahua were still cuddled up, resting.

"Maizie opened the back door!" Raider excitedly told the pair.

"You guys should go outside and run around for a while," Dutch suggested to the two dogs.

"No…not me," Georgie replied. "I just hope we don't get in trouble tomorrow morning when the staff shows up."

"Don't worry about that," Raider responded. "They'll probably think somebody broke into the building."

"Where's Maizie?" Peg asked.

"She's still out there somewhere," Dutch replied. "That dog has more energy than any puppy I've ever seen."

"I think I'll go back out and play with her," Raider told the others, as he happily turned and walked away.

Once the Pit Bull Terrier was gone, Dutch walked into Peg's cage and plopped down on her bed, so he would be close to the other two dogs.

A few quiet minutes passed before Raider came charging back down the walkway, barking like mad.

"She's gone!" he finally said, standing in front of Georgie's cage, panting. "The puppy is gone!"

"I doubt it," Dutch responded, unconvinced. "Did you look everywhere in the yard?"

"Yes," Raider replied emphatically. "I ran around the building three times and she's not in any of the pens!"

"Don't worry, she'll turn up," Dutch said confidently.

"I don't know," Peg interjected, sounding worried. "What if something happens to her?"

"If she gets out of the yard, she could end up on the main road," Georgie said, standing up.

"And get hit by a car!" Peg added anxiously.

"Okay, okay," Dutch said, resigned. "Let's go out and find her. But after that, unless there's food involved, consider me comatose until the morning."

Led by Raider, the pack of dogs walked the length of the walkway, through the storage room and out the exit door. Georgie and Peg sniffed around and marked spots where the other dogs had been, while Dutch followed Raider to the padlocked gate.

"She may be a crazy puppy, but I don't know how she made it out of here," Raider said, poking his snout in the small opening beneath the gate.

While Dutch wandered off to go find Georgie and Peg, the Pit Bull walked along the fence that bordered the parking lot, sniffing as he went. Just before he got to where the fence line made a turn, Raider spotted a deep hole in the ground.

"She escaped!" he cried. "She dug her way out!"

Within seconds, Georgie, Peg and Dutch were standing alongside Raider, staring at the puppy's escape route. As soon as the dogs leaned down to check out the crevice in the ground, their attention was diverted by a sound coming from beyond the fence. When they looked up they saw Maizie running across the hillside, tossing a tennis ball to herself.

The dogs barked with joy, and then one by one quickly scurried under the fence, hurrying as fast as they could to join the puppy. Once they got close, Maizie took off running and the others chased after her in a wide, looping circle.

For the first time since they were put in cages at Blithedale Animal Shelter, the old dog, whose owner had passed away; the three-legged Chihuahua, who was abandoned by her family; the Golden Retriever, who lost her family to a divorce; the Pit Bull Terrier, who lost his home because of his breed; and the puppy, who was given up for simply being a puppy, were as free and happy as dogs can be.

Not long after, Ginny woke up in the administration building and went to check on the dogs. When she spotted the open cage doors where the dogs had been housed, her heart sank. Quivering with fear, she frantically searched several of the nearby empty cages. Coming out of one of them, she looked toward the back of the building and saw the exit door open in the storage room. She ran as fast as she could outside and began desperately circling the yard, calling for the dogs at the top of her lungs.

Unable to find them and completely winded, Ginny stopped running. With her hands on her knees, thinking what to do next, she heard a noise. When she looked in the direction it was coming from, Ginny spotted the dogs happily running about on the moonlit hillside. She rushed to the fence and cupped her hands around her mouth, as if she were about to yell something. She took a breath in, but nothing came out.

Eventually Ginny would go through the front gate and corral the dogs. But for the moment she stood silent, smiling, with tears streaming down her face.

The next morning life at the shelter went on as if nothing had happened the night before. Without the usual procession of people looking for a furry companion to take home, Tom was able to give the dogs extra attention and longer stints in the playpens.

From the time Ginny returned to work until New Year's Eve, the shelter stayed pretty quiet. She took advantage of it by giving Maizie a few training lessons and catching up on long-neglected organizational stuff. But soon enough, unfortunately, dogs of every size, breed, and age began to fill the empty cages at the Blithedale Animal Shelter. Sadly, Maizie, Georgie, Raider, Peg and Dutch still remained.

Ten days into January an old friend of Ginny's named Chris Wapoot showed up at the shelter, looking for a dog. While Ginny talked to him about Dutch, the story of the five dogs escaping on Christmas Eve came up in conversation. Chris was amused by the tale and visited with each of the participants, but ultimately decided to adopt an older Lab mix named Frieda.

A week after Chris went home with his new furry friend, a co-worker of Ginny's handed her a copy of the local paper. To her surprise and delight, Chris, who was a senior writer for the paper, had taken her unusual evening with the dogs and turned it into a front page story. The headline read: "The Hillside Five Make Their Own Holiday Fun."

Word of the canine escape artists quickly spread throughout the valley, and people began coming to the shelter to see the *Hillside Five*. The day after the story appeared in the paper, a local TV news station visited the shelter to do a piece on the now-famous dogs, increasing the interest in them even more.

Within two days, Maizie, Georgie, Raider, Peg and Dutch had found homes. Maizie got adopted by a dog trainer named Sue Baker, Georgie was taken in by a family who lived on an apple farm and had three young kids; Raider got adopted by an Iraq War vet, who liked to cook; Peg got adopted by an unattached female high school guidance counselor; and Dutch got adopted by the owner of a country inn with a great big fireplace, where he is now the lounger-in-chief.

Experience the Tail-Wagging World of Mark Asher

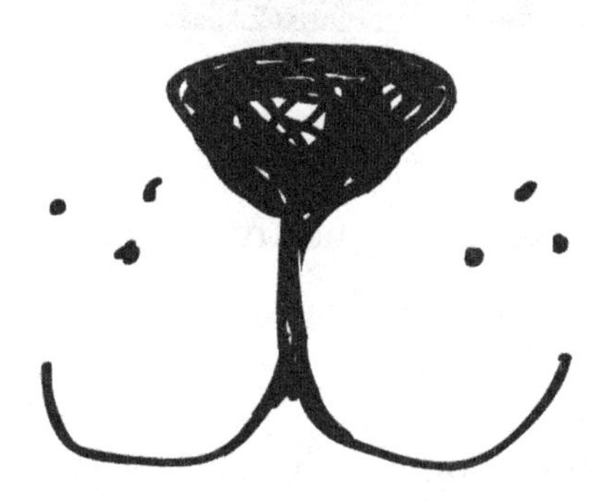

Narrated by a rescue dog that ends up in a home for seniors. A heartwarming story with over 400 five-star reviews.

"The reader won't easily forget Wrigley, a dog who gives his whole heart to bringing out the best in people."
—*Susan Wilson, New York Times bestselling author of One Good Dog*

Courtney Cromwell searches for her lost chocolate Lab and learns important life lessons.

"A wise and warm-hearted fable about the Rainbow Bridge and all the doggie delights that lie beyond it."

—*Best Friends Magazine*

Stunning duotone portraits of senior dogs along with their longevity secrets.

"These animals jump from the pages, warm the heart, and inspire the soul."
—*The Humane Society of the United States*

A moving memoir that will soothe the heartache of anyone whose lost a beloved four-legged companion.

"The honesty and wisdom that grace this book will serve as a balm for others coping with their own pain."

—*Best Friends Magazine*